Stella AND THE Night Sprites

Tooth Bandits

By Sam Hay

Illustrated by Lisa Manuzak

BRANCHES

SCHOLASTIC INC.

Read all about
Stella AND THE Night Sprites!

Table of Contents

For Alice and Archie, my own wee Sprites, who always see the magic in everything. – SH
For Pepper the Cat, who has seen me through everything and will be with me always. – LM

Text copyright © 2016 by Sam Hay
Illustrations copyright © 2016 by Scholastic Inc.

Library of Congress Cataloging-in-Publication Data
Hay, Sam, author.
  Tooth bandits / by Sam Hay. — First edition.
    pages cm. — (Stella and the night sprites; 2)
    Summary: Stella hopes to use her magic glasses to see the Tooth Fairy, but instead she sees Piper, the Tooth Bandit, a type of night sprite that steals the coins left for children and uses them to decorate their scooters—so Stella comes up with a different kind of decoration for the bandits.
    ISBN 0-545-82000-6 (pbk. : alk. paper) — ISBN 0-545-82001-4 (hardcover: alk. paper) — ISBN 0-545-82006-5 (ebook) — ISBN 0-545-82007-3 (eba ebook)
    1. Tooth Fairy (Legendary character)—Juvenile fiction. 2. Fairies—Juvenile fiction. 3. Eyeglasses—Juvenile fiction. 4. Magic—Juvenile fiction. 5. Teeth— Juvenile fiction. [1. Tooth Fairy—Fiction. 2. Fairies—Fiction. 3. Eyeglasses—Fiction. 4. Magic—Fiction. 5. Teeth—Fiction.] I. Title.
    PZ7.1.H39To 2016
    813.6—dc23
    [Fic]
                              2015011358

ISBN 978-0-545-82001-1 (hardcover)/ISBN 978-0-545-82000-4 (paperback)

10 9 8 7 6 5 4 3 2 1   16 17 18 19 20

Printed in China   38
First edition, January 2016
Illustrated by Lisa Manuzak
Edited by Katie Carella
Book design by Liz Herzog

1

Sleepover Surprise

Stella picked up a cupcake. *"Mmmm,"* she said. "This looks so yummy."

"So do my hands!" Her friend Beth wiggled her fingers. They were covered in chocolate frosting!

Stella and her friends Beth and Emily were having a sleepover at Beth's house. Beth's mom had helped them bake cupcakes.

"*Whoa!*" Emily yelled as something gray and fluffy jumped onto the table. "Cookie wants a cupcake, too."

Beth laughed. "Cats don't eat cupcakes!"

"Cats don't climb on the table, either!" Beth's mom added. She plunked him on the floor. "Eat up, girls! It's almost bedtime."

Beth took a bite of her cupcake. "*Ow!*" She put her hand to her mouth. "My tooth feels like it might fall out."

"Wiggle it," Emily said. "That's what *I* did. Mine came out really quickly."

"I've got a wobbly tooth, too," Stella said. "See?"

Emily looked at Stella's tooth, then back at Beth. "I wonder whose tooth will fall out first?"

Stella hoped it would be hers. Then she might get to meet the Tooth Fairy. Ever since Stella got her new glasses, she'd been able to see night sprites. Stella knew fairies were different from night sprites. But she wondered if her magic glasses might work on fairies, too.

All of a sudden, Beth gasped. "My tooth! It fell out!"

"Already? Let me see . . ." Beth's mom bent down to look. "Oh! That's such a clean, white tooth!"

Beth smiled. "I hope the Tooth Fairy gives me a really shiny coin for it!"

"Well, you had better get to bed," her mom said, "or she won't have time to leave anything!"

Stella thought about the Tooth Fairy as the girls got ready for bed. *Maybe I'll get to meet her when she comes for Beth's tooth!*

"I wonder what the Tooth Fairy does with the teeth?" Stella asked.

"My mom says she builds fairy castles with them," Beth said, climbing into bed.

"My sister says she turns them into necklaces," Emily said.

Beth put her tooth under her pillow. "I'm going to stay awake and ask her."

"Me, too," Emily said. She yawned. Beth yawned, too.

But Stella wasn't tired. She was excited! She made sure her glasses were on extra tight.

When Stella first found out her glasses were magic, she wondered if she should tell her friends about them. But she wasn't sure the magic would work for anyone else. And secretly, she liked having something special that was just for her.

The girls said good night and lay quietly in the dark. Then Beth spoke up. "What do you think the Tooth Fairy looks like?"

"I think she has beautiful silver wings," Stella said. "And a long gold dress and a sparkly purse for her coins."

"Uh-huh," Beth mumbled sleepily.

Stella waited for her friends to say something else. But the room was quiet. They had fallen asleep.

Must stay awake, Stella told herself. But her eyes were beginning to close . . .

A puff of cool air brushed Stella's nose. She woke up. It felt much later, now. The moon was shining in through the curtains. Stella looked around. That's when she saw it: a tiny light glowing under Beth's pillow. *Oh!* Stella gasped. *The Tooth Fairy!*

2

Sprite Light

Stella stared at the tiny light. She didn't dare breathe. *If the Tooth Fairy knows I can see her, she might fly away*, Stella thought.

Just then, the light shot out from under Beth's pillow and zipped across the room. Stella leaned forward to get a better look. Her glasses felt warm and tingly.

Huh? The light was coming from a little yellow scooter, the size of Stella's thumb. And a teeny girl in a silver-and-yellow jumpsuit was riding the scooter! Stella rubbed her eyes. *The Tooth Fairy rides a scooter?*

Stella took a deep breath. "Hi!" she whispered.

The scooter skidded to a halt in midair. Stella could see yellow wings at the bottom of the scooter flapping backward and forward. The tiny girl had wings, too. Silver wings with sparkly orange tips. The girl peered out at Stella from under her silver helmet.

"Can you *see* me?" the girl asked. Her bright blue eyes blinked in surprise.

"Yes." Stella nodded.

The girl frowned. "But humans can never see us."

"I can. I have special glasses," Stella said. "Are you the Tooth Fairy?"

The girl giggled. "No, silly!"

"Oh," Stella said. "Are you a night sprite then?"

The girl's eyes widened. "Yeah," she said. "How did you know?"

"I've seen sprites before," Stella said. She peered at the girl. *You look a lot like Trixie*, she thought. Trixie was the knit-knotter

TRIXIE

night sprite Stella had met the other night. This sprite was the same size as Trixie. She had wings like Trixie, too—and the same sparkly glow around her. But Trixie didn't ride a flying scooter. Then Stella spotted something else. On the front of this girl's scooter was a basket with a coin inside.

"Wait a minute," Stella said, "if you're *not* the Tooth Fairy, then why do you have a coin in your basket?"

"Not telling!" The sprite giggled again.

A bad thought popped into Stella's mind. She said it out loud. "Did you TAKE my friend Beth's coin?"

"It's not Beth's coin anymore," the girl said. "It's mine now!" Then she turned and zoomed away.

"Hey!" Stella whispered. "That's not fair! Wait!"

But the sprite was heading for the door.

Stella wriggled out of her sleeping bag. "Come back! Oh!" She stumbled. Stella had almost stepped on Emily!

The sprite giggled.

Stella wagged her finger at the sprite. "You stole Beth's coin! Put it back!"

"No!" The sprite stuck out her tongue. Then she zipped out into the hall.

Purrfect Timing!

Stella had to do something fast. But the sprite could have gone anywhere! Beth's house had plenty of places to hide.

Stella slipped out into the hall. Without the moonlight, she couldn't see anything. Stella felt butterflies in her tummy.

What if the sprite went into Beth's parents' room? Stella thought. *I can't go in there!*

Just then, Stella spotted the sprite's tiny glow at the end of the hall. It was coming from behind a frame over on the table. Stella crept toward the light and peeked around the side of the frame.

"*Eeee!*" the sprite shot out and zoomed over Stella's head. Her yellow scooter wings flapped. And the sprite's own wings flapped, too! Two sets of wings made her fly even faster than before.

"Get back here!" Stella whispered.

The sprite whooshed past Beth's parents' bedroom door. She zipped into Beth's baby brother's room.

Stella tiptoed after her. "Give back Beth's coin!" she said.

"No!" the sprite shouted.

Stella tried to grab the sprite. *"Ow!"* She tripped over a toy. The sprite took her chance and darted ahead.

But then, a streak of gray fur jumped out of the shadows.

MEOOWWW!

"Cookie!" Stella gasped.

The cat's tail twitched. His claws were out. His yellow eyes were big and round—and they were looking at the sprite.

Can cats see night sprites? Stella wondered. Then . . .

Meoow! Cookie sprang at the sprite.

The tiny girl did an amazing loop-the-loop move to fly back into the hallway. But the coin tumbled out of her basket. Stella jumped to grab it.

"Got it!" Stella said.

The sprite buzzed angrily around Stella's head. "That's my coin!"

"No, it's not!" Stella ran back down the hall and quickly—but quietly—closed the bedroom door.

Scaredy-Cat

Stella looked at her friends. *Phew!* They were both still asleep. She gently pushed the coin under Beth's pillow. *Huh? Something else was under there!* Stella pulled out a small red pencil sharpener. *What's this doing under Beth's pillow?*

Stella jumped as a puff of cool air brushed the back of her neck. The little scooter sprite buzzed past her nose. *Oh no!* Stella thought. *I must not have shut the door all the way!*

"Give me back that shiny coin!" the sprite squealed.

"You shouldn't take things that don't belong to you," Stella whispered.

"I didn't *take* the coin!" the sprite yelled. "I swapped it." She pointed to the sharpener in Stella's hand.

"You mean you swapped the coin for *this*?" Stella asked. "A pencil sharpener isn't the same as—"

Just then, there was a scratch at the door. It creaked open more and Cookie padded in. The sprite zoomed up to the ceiling.

Cookie jumped on Beth's bed. He sat there, looking up at the sprite. His tail twitched.

The sprite stuck out her tongue. "Yucky cat!" Then she called down to Stella, "Make him go away!"

"I can't," Stella said. "Cookie sleeps on Beth's bed."

"*Aww,* that's not fair," the sprite whined. "Then *I'll* have to go." She pouted. Then she looked right at Stella. "I'll see you again soon—when *your* tooth falls out!"

Stella felt her tooth. It was very wobbly!

The sprite did a giant loop-the-loop in the air and made a glittery circle. Then *ZIP!* She zoomed through the middle of it, and was gone.

Cookie curled up into a ball at the end of Beth's bed. Stella slipped back into her sleeping bag. She sighed. *I wish I'd seen the Tooth Fairy instead of that mean sprite.* She looked over at the cat. "At least the sprite won't come back with you here, Cookie," she whispered. *But what if she comes to my house when MY tooth falls out?*

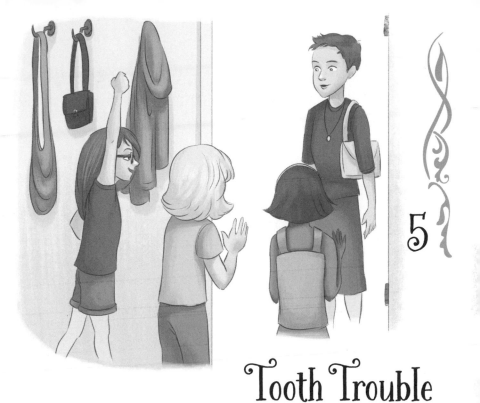

Tooth Trouble

*D*INGDONG!

Stella, Beth, and Emily raced to answer the front door. It was the next morning and the girls had been trying to guess whose mom would come to collect her first—Stella's or Emily's.

"Mom!" Stella yelled.

"You won!" Emily grinned.

"Hi, honey!" Stella's mom hugged her tight. "Did you girls have a great time?"

"Yeah!" cried Stella.

"Look what we made," Emily said. She held up a paper bag with Stella's name on it.

Stella's mom peeked inside. "Cupcakes!" She smiled. "My favorite."

"And guess what else happened!" Beth grinned and showed the gap where her tooth had been. "And look what the Tooth Fairy left under my pillow!" She held out her coin.

"Wow!" Mom turned to Beth's mom. "I think Stella might be getting a visit from the Tooth Fairy soon, too. Her tooth has been loose for days."

Stella gulped. She didn't want a visit from the Tooth Fairy. Not yet, anyway. First she had to figure out how she would keep her coin safe from that sprite!

Stella said good-bye to her friends and climbed into the car. She couldn't stop thinking about her sprite problem. She wondered if she should borrow her big brother, Josh's, money box. It had a real lock and key. *But,* she thought, *if I hide my tooth in there then the Tooth Fairy might not be able to find it, either!*

"Are you worried about your tooth?" Mom asked as she drove out of Beth's driveway.

"Well, sort of," Stella mumbled.

"Then how about a quick stop at the bead store?" Mom said. "It might take your mind off your wobbly tooth."

Stella smiled. "Oh! Yes, please!" Then an idea popped into Stella's head. The lady who owned the bead store was special. She had turned Stella's glasses into magic glasses! *She knows all about night sprites,* Stella thought. *Maybe she can tell me how to stop that sneaky sprite from taking my coin!*

Bells and Whistles

Stella raced inside the store. "Wow!" she said under her breath. The beads all looked amazing. They glittered in hundreds of little trays. There were seashell beads. Moon beads. Pretty pink flower beads. Beads shaped like bunnies. And some beads that looked like mirrors. Stella could see her face in them. Another tray held beads shaped like musical instruments: flutes, drums, and violins!

"Oh, look," Mom said, waving to another customer. "It's my friend Jenny from work. I should say hi."

But Stella wasn't listening. She had smelled something sweet in the air. *Strawberries!* The air always smelled like strawberries when the magic lady was close by. Stella's heart beat faster. She glanced around. The lady was stocking shelves at the back of the store.

Stella walked up to her. "*Um—er*—hi!" Stella said.

The lady turned. "Oh, hi, Stella!"

Stella blinked. The lady looked so colorful! Her skirt shone with gold twinkles. Her tights were raspberry pink with silver spots. Her top shimmered silver. And there was a warm twinkly glow around her.

Stella suddenly felt shy. The lady knew *her* name. But she didn't know the lady's name.

"My name's Clara Bell, by the way," the lady said. "But, please, just call me Clara."

Stella gasped. *Did Clara read my mind?*

Clara's green eyes sparkled. "How are your new glasses?"

"Awesome!" Stella touched the frames. Her glasses grew warmer. Her face felt tingly.

"And have you met any new *friends?*" Clara asked with a wink.

Stella knew Clara must have been talking about the night sprites. "Well, yes . . ." she began. "I met a new sprite last night. But she wasn't as friendly as Trixie."

"Really?" Clara looked worried.

"She tried to take my friend's coin," Stella explained.

"Oh, dear," Clara said. "That's not very nice. What did this sprite look like?"

"She had silver wings with orange tips," Stella explained. "And she rode a tiny scooter."

"*Ah!*" Clara nodded. "You met a tooth bandit."

"A tooth bandit?"

"Yes, they're clever sprites," Clara said. "Did she show you some scooter tricks?"

Stella nodded. "Yes, the sprite looped around a lot. But why did she take Beth's coin? And how can I make sure she doesn't take mine?"

"Well—" Clara was about to reply, when Mom walked over.

"Look, Stella!" Mom said. "I found these sparkly sequins for you."

"Thanks, Mom," Stella said.

Clara reached into her skirt pocket. "And here's something else for you, Stella." She held out a tiny bead. "It's for being such a good customer."

"Thanks!" Stella said. The bead was a little silver whistle.

"That's so kind of you," Mom said.

Clara smiled. Then she leaned down. "This is a special bead, Stella. I think you might find it *very* handy!" She winked.

Loose Tooth

$\mathcal{S}$tella looked at the whistle bead on the way home. It felt warm in her hand. *What did Clara mean about this bead being handy?* Stella wondered. *I wish Clara had told me how to stop the tooth bandit from taking my coin.* She sighed.

Stella's tooth felt really loose, now. She tried extra hard not to wobble it. During dinner, she didn't chew near her loose tooth. She said no to a crunchy cookie for dessert. And when she was watching TV with Josh, she didn't wiggle it at all. Not once!

But at bedtime she bumped it with her toothbrush. *"Ow!"* She put her hand up to her mouth. The bump had made her tooth feel like it was about to . . .

"My tooth!" Stella looked in the mirror.

Josh rushed into the bathroom. He peered inside Stella's mouth. "*Whoa*, you've got the BIGGEST gap ever. Mom! Dad!" he shouted. "Stella's tooth fell out!"

"Yay! Your first tooth!" Mom said, running in. Pepper the dog bounded in, too.

"No, Pepper!" Stella giggled, holding her tooth out of the dog's reach.

"It looks shiny," Dad said. "The Tooth Fairy will need to wear sunglasses tonight!"

Stella smiled nervously. She was already thinking about the tooth bandit!

Stella hugged Pepper tightly. *I wish Mom would let you sleep on my bed*, she thought. *Then the tooth bandit might stay away!*

While Dad took Pepper back to the kitchen, Stella headed to her bedroom.

"I have something for you," Mom said, sitting down on Stella's bed. She held out a tiny pink purse.

"It's a Tooth-Fairy pocket. You put your tooth inside. See, like this." Mom slid Stella's tooth into the pocket and put it under her pillow. "In the morning your tooth will be gone. And you'll find a shiny coin inside."

"*Um*—thanks." Stella wasn't sure there would be a coin in the pocket in the morning. Not if the tooth bandit had her way!

"Now, into bed and straight to sleep," Mom said. She took Stella's glasses off and put them by her bed. "Night, Stella." Mom turned off the light.

"Night, Mom," Stella called. But she wasn't going to sleep. *I'm going to stay up to meet the Tooth Fairy. And I'm going to stop that tricky sprite from taking my coin!* Stella put her glasses back on. She lay in the dark for a while. *Stay awake!* She told herself. But her eyes felt heavy. Soon, she drifted off.

THUMP!

Stella blinked and sat up. Something heavy had fallen off her desk. Her room was much darker now. Stella heard a rustling noise on the floor. "My pencil case! How did it get down there?" A silver light was moving around inside the case. *Ooo*, Stella thought. *I hope it's the Tooth Fairy!* She frowned. *But why would the Tooth Fairy be inside my pencil case?* Then Stella spotted something else . . .

A scooter! Stella groaned. That meant one thing. The tooth bandit!

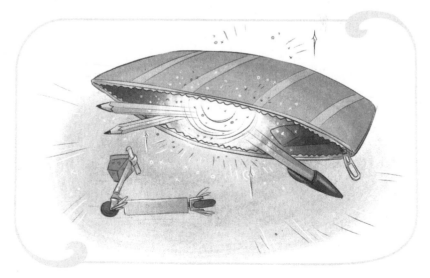

Trade-Off

Stella grabbed under her pillow. She pulled out the little purse. *If the tooth bandit is here,* she thought, *then the Tooth Fairy must have already visited!* Stella opened the purse. A shiny coin sat inside. *Phew! My coin's still here,* Stella thought. *But I can't believe I missed meeting the Tooth Fairy again.* She slid the purse back under her pillow. *That tooth bandit is not going to take my coin!*

Stella could see a pair of tiny legs poking out of the pencil case. Stella felt a bubble of anger in her belly. *The tooth bandit's taking my pens, too? We'll just see how she likes it when someone takes HER stuff!*

Stella crept out of bed. She picked up the bandit's scooter.

BEEP BEEP BEEP! A little alarm sounded.

"Hey!" came a voice from inside the pencil case. The tooth bandit shuffled out. In her arms was a paper clip. "Give me back my scooter!"

"Not until you stop taking MY things," Stella said.

"I'm not *taking* your things!" the sprite cried. "I was looking for something good to swap for your coin."

Stella looked at the paper clip. "You can't swap THAT for my coin!"

"Why not?" the sprite asked. Her shoulders drooped. Her bottom lip started to wobble.

Stella handed back her scooter. "Because that's also mine. And because a paper clip is—well, it's a paper clip. It's not nearly as good as a coin," Stella said.

"B-b-b-but I *need* your coin," the tooth bandit sniffled. "F-f-f-for my s-s-s-scooter!" Little sparkly tears fell down her cheeks.

"Please don't cry," Stella said. She wiped the sprite's tears with her pajama sleeve.

"But you don't understand," the sprite cried. "I'm the *only* tooth bandit who doesn't have a coin on her scooter."

"Huh?"

"Tooth bandits decorate their scooters with fairy coins," the sprite explained.

"Oh," Stella said. *So that's why she wants my coin!*

"But I don't have any coins," the sprite cried. "My scooter is plain."

Stella remembered how she had put streamers on her own bike last week to make it look cooler. "How do tooth bandits know where to find coins? Do you follow the Tooth Fairy around?"

"No, silly!" the bandit said. "When a child puts a tooth under her pillow, her window lights up with fairy dust. We follow the light!"

"Then you go and take the coins?"

The bandit nodded. "We go and *swap* the coins. Only—" The sprite looked sad again. "Somehow I always pick houses with cats in them. I'm scared of cats."

"Well, you're lucky I don't have a cat," Stella said. "But swapping coins for paper clips isn't a fair trade."

"Why not? They're both shiny," the sprite said. "See?"

The sprite wiggled the paper clip. It shimmered in the light.

"Wait a minute—" A slow smile spread over Stella's face. "I've got an idea!"

9

A Wheelie Good Idea

Stella carried the paper clip over to a little set of pink drawers. "Fly over here," she called to the sprite. "I'm Stella, by the way. What's your name?"

"Piper!" the sprite said, landing on the set of drawers.

"Cool name," Stella said.

Piper blushed. "*Um*—thanks."

"This is where I keep some of *my* shiny things," Stella said as she opened the top drawer.

"Ooo," Piper squealed. "So sparkly!"

"I love shiny stuff," Stella said. "I keep shimmery paper and glitter in this drawer. And in here"—Stella opened the next drawer—"I keep sequins and stickers."

"Wow!" Piper said, looking down into the drawer. *"Oops! W-w-whoa!"* Piper had leaned so far forward, she fell off the edge and landed in a pile of sequins.

"Do you want to sit on my shoulder?" Stella asked.

"Okay!" Piper flew up and landed on Stella's shoulder.

Stella smiled. "Now look at these stickers." She pulled out a sheet of gold stars. "Mom used to stick them on my reward chart."

Piper cocked her head to one side. "What's a *reward chart*?"

"A chart to help you to remember to do stuff. Like, make your bed," Stella said.

"Tooth bandits don't have beds," Piper said. "We sleep on our scooters."

Stella giggled. *Mom definitely wouldn't let me sleep on my bike!*

"Well, these are leftover stickers," Stella said. "Want to stick some on your scooter?"

"Yes, please," Piper said.

Stella peeled off a gold star. Then Piper stuck it on her scooter basket.

"And look over here," Stella said, opening a box on her desk. "This is my bead box."

"So bright!" Piper exclaimed. "So sparkly!"

"Me and my sprite friend, Trixie, call them *sparkles*," Stella said, running her fingers through the beads. "These gold beads would look amazing on the handlebars of your scooter."

"Oh, yes!" Piper said, clapping her hands.

"We can add glitter streamers, too," Stella went on, picking up colorful ribbons. "They blow in the wind when you ride. And see this paper clip"—she held up the one Piper had found—"we can shine it up like this." Stella rubbed it on her pajama top. Then she twisted the clip into a heart shape and tied it to the front of Piper's scooter.

"YAY!" Piper cried.

Ping! Ping! Ping!

The sprite's wings lit up. Tiny glittery wheel shapes fizzled like firecrackers.

"Wow!" Stella blinked. "What just happened?"

Piper giggled. "Those are my happy wheels!" she said. "Tooth bandits have wheels on their wings. They light up when we are having fun!"

Ping!

"Awesome," Stella said. "I wish I had wheelie wings, too!"

"Thank you for making my scooter look amazing," Piper said.

"We're only getting started!" Stella took out a glue stick. "Should we add some silver sequins?"

Suddenly, a bright pink bubble filled the air above their heads.

POP!

Pink glitter rained down on Stella and Piper.

Sparkle Friends

Stella and Piper gasped as a curly-haired sprite popped out of the pink bubble.

"Trixie!" Stella cried. "I'm so glad you're here!"

Trixie did three forward rolls in the air. She landed on top of the craft drawers. "Hi, Stella! How are you?"

"Great!" Stella laughed.

"Who is this?" Trixie smiled at Piper.

The tooth bandit shuffled her feet.

"This is my new friend, Piper," Stella said.

"Hi, Piper!" Trixie waved. Then she spotted Piper's scooter. "You're a tooth bandit?"

"*Um*—yeah," Piper said quietly.

"I've heard that tooth bandits can do supercool scooter tricks!" Trixie said.

"Yeah," Stella said. "You should see Piper ride. She is so fast!"

The tooth bandit blushed. "Thanks."

"Well," Trixie said. "I only popped in to say hi! Now I have to run to a knot-athon!"

"A *what*-athon?" Stella asked.

"A *knot*-athon! It's a knit-knotter contest to see which sprite can tie the most knots."

Stella remembered how Trixie and the other knit-knotters could tie superduper knots. They used to tie them in children's hair when they were asleep. But not anymore! Stella had shown the sprites how to tie knots in *dolls'* hair instead.

"For tonight's knot-athon, we're using a bunch of neon Halloween wigs we found in an old attic!" Trixie said.

"Fun!" Stella smiled.

"Gotta go!" Trixie said. She looked at Piper. "By the way, I LOVE your scooter decorations! Bye, Piper. Bye, Stella."

A pink bubble appeared around Trixie. *POP!* She was gone.

Piper looked a bit worried. "I'm glad Trixie likes my scooter decorations. But I'm not sure the other tooth bandits will like them."

"I'm sure they will," Stella said.

"But my scooter looks different. What if they laugh at me?" she asked.

"They won't laugh," Stella said. "Maybe the other tooth bandits could style their scooters this way, too."

Piper didn't look so sure.

"You should call some of your friends over," Stella suggested. "We can show them how cool your scooter looks."

Piper shook her head. "I don't really have any friends."

"Why not?" Stella asked.

Piper shrugged. "I guess I'm a bit shy."

"Huh?" Stella said. "You weren't shy when you took Beth's coin!"

Piper blushed. "Well I *really* wanted that coin! But making friends is hard."

Stella nodded. She wished she could call up some tooth bandits—and help Piper make friends. *But how do you get in touch with night sprites?* Stella wondered.

Just then, something shiny caught Stella's eye: the silver whistle bead that Clara had given her. Stella gasped. It was glowing!

"I wonder . . ." Stella picked up the bead. It felt warm and tingly. *Just like how my glasses feel when I see Clara and the night sprites,* Stella thought. "A special friend of mine said this bead would come in handy," Stella told Piper. "It must be a *magic* bead! I wonder what will happen if . . ."

Stella put the whistle to her lips and blew.

Scooter Scramble

The whistle didn't make any sound. So Stella blew it again. Harder.

"TOO LOUD!" Piper squeaked with her hands over her ears. "STOP!"

"But I don't hear anything." Stella frowned.

All of a sudden, there was a loud *WHIZZ FIZZZZ* noise! Dozens of sparkly loop-the-loop circles popped up around the room. A sprite jumped out of each circle.

"Tooth bandits!" Stella cried. There were lots of them. They lit up the room like Christmas lights!

Most of the sprites wore sparkly, colorful jumpsuits. Some had glittery pants. All of them rode scooters. And they all had coins stuck to their scooters.

A sprite on a shiny purple scooter buzzed past Stella's face, just missing her glasses. "*Whoa!*" Stella said, stepping back.

Another sprite in a silver jumpsuit spun around and around above Stella's head. Stella looked up. The sprite's scooter changed color every few seconds. *Blue. Green. Orange!*

"*WEEEEEEE!*" a super-fast sprite zoomed down Stella's curtains. Four more raced after that sprite.

"Watch it!" Stella called as two pink scooters zipped between her feet. "Slow down!"

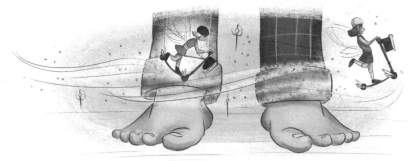

But the sprites didn't slow down. They went racing and chasing around the room— doing somersaults and wheelies!

ZOOOM!
WHOOSH!
WHIZZ!

Stella felt dizzy watching them. She picked up the whistle and blew.

The scooters screeched to a stop as the sprites covered their ears. Some hovered in the air. Others landed on Stella's desk.

"S-s-s-sorry about that. H-h-hello, everyone, I'm Stella!"

Dozens of bright eyes stared back at her. "You can see us?" a tooth bandit asked.

"Yes," Stella said. "And I love all your scooters!"

The sprites whispered to one another.

A tall tooth bandit with a super-shiny coin on her helmet fluttered near Stella. *She looks like the leader of the group,* Stella thought. "Why did you call us here?" the tooth bandit asked.

"I wanted to show you something." Stella looked around for Piper. But she couldn't see her anywhere.

"What did you want to show us?" the tall tooth bandit asked. She drummed her fingers on her scooter handlebars. "Come on! We're in a hurry! We've got coins to find!"

Stella gulped. *Do they know there's a coin under my pillow?*

Stella looked around for Piper. But she still couldn't see her.

The sprites began to fidget.

"I want you to meet my new friend," Stella said. "Only I don't know where she went."

The tooth bandits' leader puffed out her cheeks. "We're leaving!" she said.

"Wait!" Stella said. "I want to show you a new way to decorate your scooters. Then you won't need to take Tooth-Fairy coins anymore!"

"*What?*" The tooth bandits gasped.

"No coins?" a green-haired sprite yelled.

"No way!" another sprite shouted.

"Shiny coins forever!" a golden-haired sprite squealed.

The tooth bandits' leader glared at Stella. "Let's go!" she called to the others.

Just then there was a screech of wheels. *FFFZZZZIIIIP!*

Something sparkly zipped across the room.

Pipe Up, Piper!

A super-shiny scooter, covered in sequins and glitter, whizzed through the air.

"Piper!" Stella cried. "There you are!"

Some sprites pointed. Others just stared.

"That tooth bandit doesn't have any coins on her scooter!" a sprite shouted.

Piper screeched to a halt. She took a deep breath. "I-I-I don't need coins," she stammered. "My friend, Stella, showed me a different way to style my scooter."

The tooth bandits looked at one another as their leader scooted right up to Piper. She looked closely at Piper's scooter. She looked it up and down. And all around. Then the tooth bandit turned to the others. A wide smile spread across her face. "This scooter is very different, but it is SUPER SHINY!" she shouted.

"I want *my* scooter to look like that!" another tooth bandit yelled.

Suddenly, the tooth bandits all crowded around Piper.

"I love your glittery sparkles!"

"Where did you get that silver heart?"

"Those gold beads shine brighter than our coins!"

A tooth bandit zoomed over to Stella. "Can you help me take the coins off my scooter, please?" she asked.

"Sure," Stella said.

"I want my scooter to look like hers," the sprite added, pointing at Piper.

All the tooth bandits began to line up next to Stella's craft drawers. While they rummaged through the sequins, Stella stacked their coins on the desk. *I hope the Tooth Fairy comes to collect all these coins,* she thought.

"*Um*—Stella," Piper called. "Do you have more paper clips? I'd like to show everyone how you made the heart."

Stella dug several paper clips out of her pencil case.

Soon, the tooth bandits were zooming around the room showing off their new scooter styles. Sequins. Streamers. Beads! Some had paper-clip shapes hanging on the front. Others had glitter ribbons dangling from their handlebars. One sprite had clipped a long chain of paper clips to the back of her scooter. It twinkled and jangled as she flew past.

But Piper wasn't joining in. She was sitting on Stella's pencil case, resting her chin on her hands.

"What's wrong?" Stella asked.

Piper sighed. "I wish I could be friends with them."

"Why can't you?"

Piper shrugged. "I don't know how to *make* friends. I mean, I've seen some of the tooth bandits before. But I've never really spoken to them."

"When I first joined Girl Scouts I didn't know ANY of the girls!"

"Really?" Piper asked.

"Sure!" Stella said. "But we played this game called Fruit Salad. I didn't know the game, so I ran the wrong way. I crashed into Beth, and *she* bumped into Emily! We all fell down. But that's how we became friends. See? Here's our photo from that day."

Piper giggled. "That is a funny way to make friends."

"Games are awesome—even when you mess up!" Stella said. "Why don't you zoom around with the other tooth bandits? It looks so fun."

Piper sighed. "I don't know."

If only Trixie were here, Stella thought, *she'd get Piper to join in.* Then Stella remembered Trixie was at the knot-athon with her friends. *The knot-athon!* Suddenly, an idea sprouted in Stella's mind. She picked up the whistle bead. *I hope this works!*

Stunt-athon

Stella blew the whistle bead. The tooth bandits stopped what they were doing. Some of them had their hands over their ears.

"Sorry again," Stella said. "But I've just had the BEST idea! We're going to hold a stunt-athon!"

"Huh?" The sprites looked at one another.

"What is a *stunt-a-thump?*" the tooth bandits' leader asked.

Stella laughed. "It's a *stunt-aTHON!* We are going to play games so you guys can show off your best scooter stunts."

"We love doing stunts!" a sprite shouted as she backflipped her scooter.

"Neat trick!" Stella said. "Everyone who takes part in the stunt-athon gets a gold-star sticker. And my friend Piper will go first."

"I don't know—" Piper began.

"You can do it, Piper!" a sprite in a gold helmet shouted.

"First up is an obstacle race. I just need some things—" Stella began hunting around her room for obstacles. She laid out an old sneaker. Her pencil case. A bouncy ball. A wooden Russian doll. And some tiny fences she found in her old farm play set.

Piper's heart was racing. "*Um*—maybe someone else should go first—" she began.

"Go, Piper!" everyone cheered.

Stella crossed her fingers for good luck as she started a countdown. "Five, four, three . . ."

Fairy Dreams

Piper took a deep breath. Then . . .

WHOOSH!

She took off.

Piper zoomed across the floor. She somersaulted over the sneaker, zipped around the doll, and bunny-hopped her scooter in and out of the fences. As Piper backflipped across the finish line, everyone cheered.

"Thanks, guys!" Piper blushed. *Ping! Ping! Ping! Ping!* All the wheel shapes on her wings lit up at once!

The stunt-athon had lots of other games, too. Scooter-skipping. Scooter-jumps! Even a scooter treasure hunt. There was scooter-tag, too. And a final showstopper, where all the sprites showed off their favorite stunts.

The tooth bandits' leader did a triple-jump somersault.

Piper was even more amazing. She did a super-fast figure-eight-double-twist!

As the last game finished, Stella was struggling to keep her eyes open. So were the tooth bandits.

Their leader raised her arm. "Time to go home!" she called. "Thanks for helping us style our scooters, Stella. And we loved the stunt-athon, too!"

Stella waved good-bye. Then the sprite leader did a giant loop-the-loop. The circle she had made lit up like a glittery-blue hoop. She jumped through the middle. *ZIP!* She was gone.

ZIP! ZIP! ZIP! The other tooth bandits left, too.

Only Piper was left. "Thanks for helping me make friends, Stella," she said. "And for making my scooter so shiny!"

"You're welcome," Stella said.

"I promise I won't take any more Tooth-Fairy coins. But"—Piper grinned—"I might come back to borrow more paper clips."

Stella smiled. "Come back any time! You can have ALL my paper clips."

"Night, Stella," Piper said. Then she did a big loop-the-loop in the air and made a blue glittery circle. *ZIP!* She zoomed through it.

Stella climbed into bed. Waves of sleepiness washed over her. She was just nodding off when a flash of gold flitted across her room. But Stella was already starting to dream.

Dear Stella,

Thank you so much for collecting
my coins from the tooth bandits.
And thank you for taking such good
care of your tooth! I've left an extra
special present, just for you. I hope
you enjoy using it to brush your teeth!

With love from,
The Tooth Fairy xx

Sam Hay lost her front tooth while eating breakfast—on picture day! Sam's aunt also decided to cut Sam's bangs that morning. So Sam's holey smile and crazy hair were captured on camera forever! Sam has never met a Tooth Fairy. But she hasn't given up hope. Whenever one of her kids loses a tooth, she sits up late with her glasses on, hoping to see one. Sam has written 30 books for children, including the Undead Pets series. She lives in Wales.

Lisa Manuzak has been wearing glasses since she was ten years old. They are definitely a magical item to help you see things, even fairies! Lisa has always loved fairies, and they were one of the first things she loved to draw when she was a kid. She would love to see a fairy in person some day. Hopefully her two cats won't keep them away!

Stella AND THE Night Sprites

~ Tooth Bandits ~

Questions and Activities

Why do Piper and the other tooth bandits take the coins the Tooth Fairy leaves behind?

What special bead does Clara give Stella? How does it help her?

Making friends can be hard. How does Stella help Piper make friends?

Imagine you are a tooth bandit. Use words and pictures to explain how you would decorate your scooter. Would you use coins? Why or why not?

There are many different types of night sprites. If you were a night sprite, which type of night sprite would you be? Write and draw your answer.